E   Porte, Barbara Ann.
POR   Harry's visit /

55A3356

DATE DUE		
NOV 9 '81		
NOV 29 '83		
FEB 23 '84		
105		

Greenwillow
Read-alone

BARBARA ANN PORTE

Harry's Visit

pictures by **YOSSI ABOLAFIA**

GREENWILLOW BOOKS · New York

Printed in the United States of America
First Edition   10 9 8 7 6 5 4 3 2 1

Library of Congress Cataloging in Publication Data

Porte, Barbara Ann.
Harry's visit.
(Greenwillow read-alone books)
Summary: Expecting he won't have a good
time, Harry visits his parents' friends.
I. Abolafia, Yossi, ill.
II. Title.   III. Series.
PZ7.P7995Har .   [E]   81-20188
ISBN 0-688-01207-8   AACR2
ISBN 0-688-01208-6 (lib. bdg.)

TO MY MOTHER AND FATHER,
DORA AND SOL PORTE
—B. A. P.

TO TAL
—Y. A.

I, Harry, am visiting.

I am visiting my Aunt Betty

and my Uncle Charlie Silverstein.

I hate visiting.

Also, they are not
my real aunt and uncle.
I just call them that to be polite.
"Always be polite, Harry,"
my father always tells me.

"Betty and Charlie," I say

under my breath.

I say it under my breath,

when no one is listening.

"They are my oldest friends,"

my father tells me.

He does not mean
that they are really old.
He means that he has known them
for a long time.

Today is just the third time
in my life that I have ever
had to see them.
I am not looking forward
to my visit.

Aunt Betty telephoned last week.

"Would Harry like to come and visit?

We would love to have him."

"Harry would like that
very much," my father said.
"Like what?" I asked my father.
My father told me.
Right away, I knew that I would not.

"Hello," Aunt Betty says,

opening the door.

I hope she will not kiss me.

She kisses me.

I wait until no one is looking,
then I wipe where she has kissed.
Germs can make diseases.
"Harry catches everything,"
my father always says.
He has not seen me
playing baseball.

"You are just in time for breakfast,"
Aunt Betty says to me.
Uncle Charlie is already at the table.
The three Silverstein children
are at the table too.

Their names are Judy, Joan,
and Jonathan.
They have a turtle
they call Joy.
I am glad I do not live here.

Aunt Betty puts French toast

in front of me.

She spoons honey over it.

At home, I put maple syrup

on my pancakes.

I do not tell her that.

"Do not be a fussy eater, Harry,"

my father always tells me.

I wish that he were here now.

"Judy, why don't you go play
with Harry?" says Aunt Betty
after breakfast.
I knew that she would say that.
I knew that she would not say,
"Jonathan, why don't you
and Harry play together?"
Sometimes I think
I must be magic.

I also think I do not want
to play with Judy.

I play with Judy.

We look at books.

We listen to her records.

I think I could be doing this

at home.

I wish I were at home.

This is turning out to be

the longest morning in my life.

"Lunchtime," says Aunt Betty.
I am glad to hear her say it.
Morning must be over.
I am glad until
I see my lunch.

Lunch is bean soup

and peanut butter sandwiches.

The peanut butter

is on pumpernickel bread.

At home, my peanut butter

is always on white bread.

"Eat what everybody else does, Harry,"

my father always tells me.

I eat my sandwich.

"Is there any chicken noodle soup?"

I ask.

No one hears me ask it.

I try the bean soup.

It tastes the way it looks.

I am not surprised.

I am very hungry, so I eat it.

That surprises me.

"Make yourself at home,"

says Uncle Charlie after lunch.

At home, we always have dessert.

"Is there something for dessert?"

I ask.

No one hears me ask it.

I ask it louder.

"Is there something for dessert?"

"Granola bars," Aunt Betty says.

She smiles at me.

"Would you like one?"

"No thank you," I tell her.

I do not tell her,

I have not ever eaten

a granola bar.

"How about an apple?"

Uncle Charlie asks.

"I bet that he would like an apple."

He puts a large apple in my face,

so I can see it and decide.

No, I decide.

I would not like it.

23

An apple all alone seems lonely.

I feel lonely.

All the Silversteins are looking at me.

I do not need so much attention.

I wait until they look away.

Then I ask in my politest voice,

"Have you any cookies?"

No one hears me ask it.

I could ask again, a little louder.

"Harry, you must speak up,"

my father sometimes tells me.

I do not ask again.

Afternoon is just beginning.

I hope it will not last

as long as lunch.

Jonathan is watching me.
He looks like he is making up
his mind.
"Harry," he asks, "do you want
to shoot some baskets with me
at the playground?"

"Mom," he asks Aunt Betty,
"can Harry come with me?"

Shoot some baskets?

He must be joking.

I am just a little taller

than one of Snow White's dwarfs.

"Yes," I say, "I would."

Maybe it will take

my mind off food.

"Sure," Aunt Betty says, "have fun.

Do not stay away too long."

I walk to the playground
with Jonathan.
At home, I cannot walk
anywhere myself.
"I will have to drive you,"
my father always says.
"It is much too far
for you to walk."

Also, at home
there is no playground.

"This is Katy, Linda, Michael,
Dennis, Mary, Mollie, Max,
and Alexander,"
Jonathan tells me
when we get there.
At home,
I just have Anthony.

32

There is a basketball court
in the playground.
It has four hoops.
Three of the hoops are very high.
One of the hoops is not so high.
"Mom made them lower it,"
says Jonathan,
"when I was your age."
Good old Aunt Betty,
I think to myself.

Jonathan throws a ball to me.

He tells me, "Practice."

He shoots a few with me,

then joins his friends.

I play with Alexander.

"Shoot," says Alexander.

I try and miss.

"Like this," says Alexander.

I try again and miss.

"One more time,"

says Alexander.

I try very, very hard.

My ball goes through the hoop.

"Hooray," says Alexander.

"Jonathan," I shout,

"I made a basket."

"Good for you," he tells me.

"I knew that you could do it."

Alexander and I take turns.

He makes a basket.

I make a basket.

Then he makes another basket.

Then I make another basket.

Sometimes we do not

make a basket.

My father will be surprised

when I tell him

how many baskets

I have made.

"Break time," says Alexander.
He and I join Jonathan
and his friends
underneath their hoop.
They are trying to decide
what we should do next.
They decide on ice cream.

We walk together
to the ice cream store.
At home, there is
no ice cream store to walk to.
We keep ice cream
in our freezer.
Ice cream from our freezer
is not as good as ice cream
from a store.
"Don't be silly, Harry,"
my father tells me
when I say that.

Everyone but me has money.
They all get allowances,
even Alexander, who's my age.
At home, my father gives me money
when he thinks I need it.

"I am treating you," says Jonathan.

"You are my guest."

I am glad to hear him say that.

Everybody gets

vanilla ice cream cones

with sprinkles.

Except Dennis gets a sundae,

and so does Alexander.

"Frozen yogurt, please,"

says Jonathan.

Only I am left.

"Me too," I say.

"I want frozen yogurt too."

I am surprised

to hear me say it.

"With sprinkles, please."

I have not ever tasted yogurt.

I taste the yogurt.

It is cold.

The sprinkles are delicious.

"Jonathan and I like yogurt,"

I tell Alexander

as we leave the store.

My father is already waiting
when Jonathan and I get back.
I am surprised to see him here
so soon.

When we get home,

I tell my father all about the visit.

"We played basketball," I say.

"I made a lot of baskets,

me and Alexander."

I tell him about Alexander.

"Alexander gets an allowance," I say.

"Everybody gets one.

Do you think

that I could get one too?"

"We will see," my father says.

"Next time," I tell my father,

"Jonathan says, next time I visit

  he will take me with him

  to play baseball.

  Jonathan says next time I visit,

  he will help me with my catching."

"I am glad you liked your visit,"

  my father says to me.

I ask him, "When will be
the next time I can visit?"
"Next time will be the next time,"
my father answers me.
"In the meantime, it is bedtime."
My father kisses me good night.
I can hardly wait for next time.
I think that maybe next time
I will take my lunch.

BARBARA ANN PORTE is the Children's Services Specialist in the Nassau Library System in New York. Her stories and poems for adults have appeared in many literary magazines throughout the country.

YOSSI ABOLAFIA was born in Tiberia, Israel. For Greenwillow he has illustrated *Buffy and Albert* by Charlotte Pomerantz. He is presently director of animation for the National Film Board of Canada.